ABOUT THE BANK STREET READY-TO-READ SERIES

More than seventy-five years of educational research, innovative teaching, and quality publishing have earned The Bank Street College of Education its reputation as America's most trusted name in early childhood education.

Because no two children are exactly alike in their development, The Bank Street Ready-to-Read series is written on three levels to accommodate the individual stages of reading readiness of children ages three through eight.

○ *Level 1:* **GETTING READY TO READ (Pre-K–Grade 1)**
Level 1 books are perfect for reading aloud with children who are getting ready to read or just starting to read words or phrases. These books feature large type, repetition, and simple sentences.

● *Level 2:* **READING TOGETHER (Grades 1–3)**
These books have slightly smaller type and longer sentences. They are ideal for children beginning to read by themselves who may need help.

○ *Level 3:* **I CAN READ IT MYSELF (Grades 2–3)**
These stories are just right for children who can read independently. They offer more complex and challenging stories and sentences.

All three levels of The Bank Street Ready-to-Read books make it easy to select the books most appropriate for your child's development and enable him or her to grow with the series step by step. The levels purposely overlap to reinforce skills and further encourage reading.

We feel that making reading fun is the single most important thing anyone can do to help children become good readers. We hope you will become part of Bank Street's long tradition of learning through sharing.

The Bank Street College of Education

To Delroy Drumgold
— B.B.

To Emily
— J.E.C.

Please visit our web site at: www.garethstevens.com
For a free color catalog describing Gareth Stevens Publishing's list
of high-quality books and multimedia programs, call 1-800-542-2595
or fax your request to (414) 332-3567.

Library of Congress Cataloging-in-Publication Data

Brenner, Barbara.
    Too many mice / by Barbara Brenner; illustrated by John Emil Cymerman.
      p. cm. -- (Bank Street ready-to-read)
    Summary: When Nita and her mother use a bunch of cats to get rid of the mice
in their house, it is only the beginning of a proliferation of animals.
    ISBN 0-8368-1771-0 (lib. bdg.)
    [1. Animals--Fiction.] I. Cymerman, John Emil, ill. II. Title. III. Series.
PZ7.B7518To   1998
[E]--dc21   97-47567

This edition first published in 1998 by
Gareth Stevens Publishing
A World Almanac Education Group Company
330 West Olive Street, Suite 100
Milwaukee, Wisconsin 53212 USA

© 1992 by Byron Preiss Visual Publications, Inc. Text © 1992 by Bank Street College
of Education. Illustrations © 1992 by John Emil Cymerman and Byron Preiss Visual
Publications, Inc.

Published by arrangement with Bantam Doubleday Dell Books For Young Readers,
a division of Bantam Doubleday Dell Publishing Group, Inc., New York, New York.
All rights reserved.

Bank Street Ready To Read™ is a registered U.S. trademark of the Bank Street Group
and Bantam Doubleday Dell Books For Young Readers, a division of Bantam Doubleday
Dell Publishing Group, Inc.

Printed in Mexico

3 4 5 6 7 8 9 06 05 04 03 02

Bank Street Ready-to-Read™

Too Many Mice

by Barbara Brenner
Illustrated by
John Emil Cymerman

A Byron Preiss Book

Gareth Stevens Publishing
A WORLD ALMANAC EDUCATION GROUP COMPANY

Nita and her mama
lived in a house
with one cat.
There was one cat,
but there were *many* mice.
Too many.

There were mice in the bedroom.
There were mice on the stairs.

There were mice in the kitchen
and mice under chairs.
There were too many mice
for one cat to catch.

"There are too many mice
in this house," said Mama.
"We need more cats."
"You are right, Mama,"
said Nita.
So Nita went looking for cats.

She ran up and down the street,
calling cats.
"Here kitty, kitty.
I know where you can find
a nice mouse dinner."

The cats came running.
A white cat,
a striped cat,

a cat with a crooked tail,
a cat with shining eyes,
and a mama cat with kittens.

The cats ran into Nita's house,
and soon all the mice ran out.

"That's better," said Mama.
"Now I will sit down
and read my paper."

But she couldn't sit down.
There was a cat in Mama's chair.
There were cats everywhere!

Nita's mama sighed.
"Now there are too many cats."
"You are right, Mama," said Nita.
"We need dogs to chase the cats."

Nita ran up and down the street.
"Here dogs, here dogs,"
she called.
"I know where you can find
lots of cats to chase."

The dogs
came running.
A black dog,
a white dog,
a big dog,
a small dog,
and a dog
with spots.
The dogs went
into the house,
and the cats
ran out!

19

"Now I can sit down and
read my paper," said Mama.
But she couldn't sit down.
A dog was in Mama's chair.
There were dogs everywhere!

"We have too many dogs,"
said Mama.
"You are right, Mama,"
said Nita.
"We need some alligators
to scare the dogs."

Nita went to the alligator pond.
"Alli, alli, gator," she called.
"I know where you can scare
some dogs!"
Two alligators popped up.

They crawled out of the pond,
down the street,
and into the house.
Snap! Snap! went their big teeth.
All the dogs ran away!

"Maybe now I can read my paper,"
said Mama.
But just then,
Snap! Snap!
An alligator ate Mama's paper.
"Alligators are worse than dogs!"
cried Mama.
"Mama, you are right,"
said Nita.
"We need an elephant
to scare the alligators."

Nita went to the zoo.
She rented an elephant.
The elephant walked into the house.
Thump! Thump!
It shook the whole house.

The alligators were scared.
They crawled down the stairs
and back to their pond.

"Now that's better,"
said Mama.
"Let's go to bed."

28

Nita and Mama lay down.
But the elephant stayed up.
Thump! Thump! Thump!
Beds shook, chairs broke,
and dishes came crashing down.

"This will not do," said Mama.
"Even one elephant is too many."
"You are right, Mama," said Nita.

"But there's only one thing
that will scare an elephant."
"What is that?" asked Mama.

31

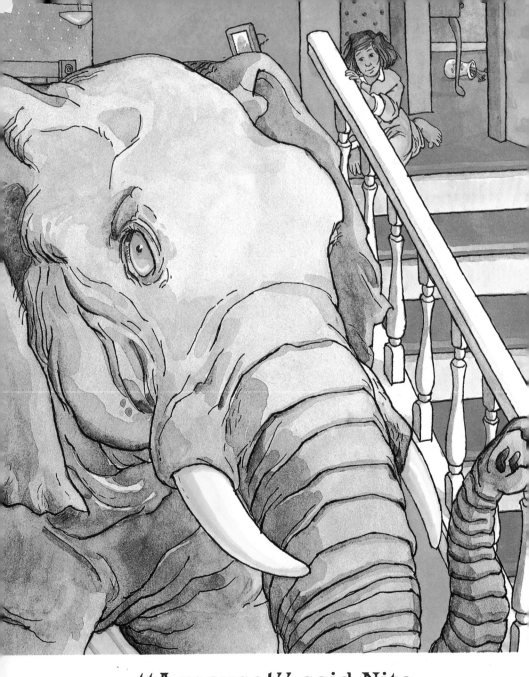

"A mouse!" said Nita.